MR. COOL

Roger Hargreaves

Written and illustrated by
Adam Hargreaves

Poor Jack Robinson wasn't feeling very well.

He had been in bed for days and he had to stay in bed until he was better.

"I'm bored," he huffed. "I wish I could go outside and play with my friends."

Suddenly, a blue blur shot in through the open window.

It looped-the-loop around the light in the ceiling and a small blue figure, wearing a hat, landed on the end of Jack's bed.

"Cool!" said Jack.

"That's me. Mr Cool," said Mr Cool.

"Cool!" repeated Jack.

"You look a bit bored," said Mr Cool. "I thought we could go and have some fun."

"I wish I could," said Jack, "but I'm not allowed out of bed."

"I think we could make an exception just this once," said Mr Cool, and he clicked his fingers.

The next instant Jack found himself sitting in the cockpit of a jet aeroplane.

"Why don't you take it out for a spin?" suggested Mr Cool.

"What? Can I really fly it?" said Jack.

"Sure you can," said Mr Cool. "It's easy!"

So Jack flew the jet-plane out across the Atlantic Ocean and back.

"That was cool," cried Jack, when they were back on the ground. "Thanks, Mr Cool!"

"We haven't finished yet," said Mr Cool and he clicked his fingers again.

Jack heard a crowd roar. He was at a football ground, but he wasn't sitting in the crowd. He was on the bench with the other players!

And he was even wearing the team strip!

"Quick!" said Mr Cool. "The manager wants you to go on."

"He wants me to play?" said Jack, incredulously. "But they're Capital United!"

And you'll never guess what . . .
Jack scored the winning goal!

"Wow! That was so cool!" said Jack.

As Jack walked off the pitch Mr Cool clicked his
fingers and whisked them away.

To climb the tallest tree in the world!

He clicked his fingers again and before you could say
Jack Robinson . . .

. . . they were standing on top of a mountain!

"Where are we?" called Jack, over the noise of the wind.

"Mount Everest!" said Mr Cool.

"How cool! What are we doing here?" shouted Jack.

"Sledging!" said Mr Cool. "Let's go!"

Jack and Mr Cool slid from the very top to the very bottom of Mount Everest.

"That was the coolest thing ever!" cried Jack.

"It was more like the c . . . c . . . coldest," stuttered Mr Cool.

For the final time that day Mr Cool clicked his fingers.

In an instant Jack found himself back in his bedroom.

"Thank you so much, Mr Cool," said Jack.
"That was . . ."

". . . amazing?!" laughed Mr Cool.

"Well, I'll be off," said Mr Cool. "But there's one more thing, Jack. Have a look in the mirror."

With this, Mr Cool shot out through the open window.

Jack went into the bathroom and looked in the mirror.

"Cool!" said Jack when he saw himself.

And why do you think Jack was so pleased?

That's right, all his spots had gone. Jack was better.

I wonder, on which page did Jack get better?

3 Great Offers for MR.MEN Fans!

MR.MEN TOKEN

1 New Mr. Men or Little Miss Library Bus Presentation Cases

A brand new stronger, roomier school bus library box, with sturdy carrying handle and stay-closed fasteners.
The full colour, wipe-clean boxes make a great home for your full collection.
They're just £5.99 inc P&P and free bookmark!

☐ MR. MEN ☐ LITTLE MISS (please tick and order overleaf)

2 Door Hangers and Posters

In every Mr. Men and Little Miss book like this one, you will find a special token. Collect 6 tokens and we will send you a brilliant Mr. Men or Little Miss poster and a Mr. Men or Little Miss double sided full colour bedroom door hanger of your choice. Simply tick your choice in the list and tape a 50p coin for your two items to this page.

PLEASE STICK YOUR 50P COIN HERE

Door Hangers (please tick)
☐ Mr. Nosey & Mr. Muddle
☐ Mr. Slow & Mr. Busy
☐ Mr. Messy & Mr. Quiet
☐ Mr. Perfect & Mr. Forgetful
☐ Little Miss Fun & Little Miss Late
☐ Little Miss Helpful & Little Miss Tidy
☐ Little Miss Busy & Little Miss Brainy
☐ Little Miss Star & Little Miss Fun

Posters (please tick)
☐ MR.MEN
☐ LITTLE MISS

CUT ALONG DOTTED LINE AND RETURN THIS WHOLE PAGE

3 Sixteen Beautiful Fridge Magnets – any **2** for **£2.00!** inc.P&P

They're very special collector's items!
Simply tick your first and second* choices from the list below
of any 2 characters!

1st Choice

☐ Mr. Happy
☐ Mr. Lazy
☐ Mr. Topsy-Turvy
☐ Mr. Bounce
☐ Mr. Bump
☐ Mr. Small
☐ Mr. Snow
☐ Mr. Wrong

☐ Mr. Daydream
☐ Mr. Tickle
☐ Mr. Greedy
☐ Mr. Funny
☐ Little Miss Giggles
☐ Little Miss Splendid
☐ Little Miss Naughty
☐ Little Miss Sunshine

2nd Choice

☐ Mr. Happy
☐ Mr. Lazy
☐ Mr. Topsy-Turvy
☐ Mr. Bounce
☐ Mr. Bump
☐ Mr. Small
☐ Mr. Snow
☐ Mr. Wrong

☐ Mr. Daydream
☐ Mr. Tickle
☐ Mr. Greedy
☐ Mr. Funny
☐ Little Miss Giggles
☐ Little Miss Splendid
☐ Little Miss Naughty
☐ Little Miss Sunshine

*Only in case your first choice is out of stock.

— TO BE COMPLETED BY AN ADULT —

**To apply for any of these great offers, ask an adult to complete the coupon below and send it with
the appropriate payment and tokens, if needed, to MR. MEN OFFERS, PO BOX 7, MANCHESTER M19 2HD**

☐ Please send ____ Mr. Men Library case(s) and/or____ Little Miss Library case(s) at £5.99 each inc P&P

☐ Please send a poster and door hanger as selected overleaf. I enclose six tokens plus a 50p coin for P&P

☐ Please send me ____ pair(s) of Mr. Men/Little Miss fridge magnets, as selected above at £2.00 inc P&P

Fan's Name _____

Address _____

_____ **Postcode** _____

Date of Birth _____

Name of Parent/Guardian _____

Total amount enclosed £_____

☐ **I enclose a cheque/postal order payable to Egmont Books Limited**

☐ **Please charge my MasterCard/Visa/Amex/Switch or Delta account** (delete as appropriate)

Card Number

Expiry date __ / __   **Signature** _____

Please allow 28 days for delivery. We reserve the right to change the terms of this offer at any time
but we offer a 14 day money back guarantee. This does not affect your statutory rights.

MR.MEN   **LITTLE MISS**
Mr. Men and Little Miss™ & ©Mrs. Roger Hargreaves

CUT ALONG DOTTED LINE AND RETURN THIS WHOLE PAGE